Emily's Room

Emily's Room

Creating Spaces

that

Unlock Your Potential

by
Katherine Allen

Illustrated by
Stephanie Mullani

Tru Publishing
2939 S Mayflower Way
Boise, ID 83709

Published by Tru Publishing. No part of this book may be reproduced or transmitted in any form or by any means, electronic or mechanical, including photocopying, recording, or by any information storage and retrieval system, without written permission from the publisher. For more information, address Tru Publishing, 2939 S Mayflower Way, Boise ID 83709. Visit the Tru Publishing website at www.TruPublishing.com

Library of Congress Control Number: 2015950779
ISBN (paperback): 978-1-941420-10-2

1 2 3 4 5 6 19 18 17 16 15
1st edition, September 2015

Printed in the United States of America

Cover and Interior Design — Tru Publishing
www.TruPublishing.com

Editing and Consulting — Aspen Morrow
www.PottengerPress.com

HAPPY CLIENTS

Under Katherine's gentle yet powerful guidance, I learned how to make seemingly small changes in my home that led to amazing transformations in my life. She integrates the physical with the spiritual seamlessly. The process was full of joy and discovery and it felt completely natural to me, even though it was my first experience with Lifestyle coaching, Feng Shui and Thriving Environments.

—Peggy J.

I pride myself on having a good eye for decorating but when I hired Katherine every room went from nice to WOW!!! She has an eye that can't be taught. Her capacity to use the things you already have in your home saved me a ton of money. Hiring Katherine is the best money I have spent.

—Cindy T.

Katherine works with beauty and energy and flow and creates amazing results. She has also enriched my personal life, enhanced my understanding of my inner life and added to my wisdom and growth. Her soul coaching has been a very positive addition to her offerings. I am a happier, wiser and more aware person thanks to her.

—Jane

Thanks Katherine! The changes we made have had a momentous effect for both my husband and me already, and I feel like we've made light years of progress. Can't wait to get to the next stage of it.

—Kerry C.

TABLE OF CONTENTS

DEDICATION

To the beauty and magic of the child within us all,
whose only desire is to bloom!

Katherine Allen

"Who am I to be brilliant, gorgeous, talented, fabulous?
Actually, who are you not to be?
We are all meant to shine, as children do..

Marianne Williamson
A Return to Love: Reflection's on the Principles of "A Course in Miracles"

MEET EMILY

Groggily, Emily awakes, wiping the sleep from her eyes. Suddenly she remembers what day it is!

Emily's hair is wired to her heart. Grinning from ear to ear causes Emily's reddish-blonde curly hair to stand up, sending out highlighted strands that look like sparklers kissed by the sun. When Emily is happy, those tiny, fiery hairs dance on top of her head, making a beautiful glow called a halo. Glimmering like diamonds in the ocean, Emily's blue-green eyes match her happy hair.

THE BIG DAY

n Saturdays, Emily gets to sleep in, but there's no time to sleep today, she is on a mission. Emily throws back the covers, jumps out of bed, and puts on her fuzzy pink slippers. Remembering her Mom's words the night before: "Em, now it's your turn to have a bigger room and decorate it any way you want, so start thinking of some ideas," she rushes into her new empty room.

LEGACIES & VISIONS

Her new room is huge and white like a blank piece of paper! The room is empty except for a full-length mirror and her favorite book. "I love my mirror!" She thinks to herself. Her grandma told her it was a magical mirror and Emily whole-heartedly agrees. She sees all kinds of things in her magic mirror. Sometimes she sees herself as a princess from a faraway place. Sometimes, when Emily twirls, she sees a beautiful white wolf who is her friend and protector.

Skipping to the big window, Emily sees the twisted and gnarled oak tree that has lived a long time. It is Emily's favorite tree—she calls it her Grandmother Tree because she can climb up in its lap. She sits there for hours dreaming about books she'll write and places she will travel.

envision

HAPPY MEMORIES

"Em, breakfast is ready," her mom calls from the kitchen.

"Coming, Mom!" Emily replies. Running to the kitchen, her favorite picture catches her eye: her family playing at the beach.

Just a glimpse of that picture makes Emily feel like she is there—watching the waves, hearing the roar as they hit the soft, warm sand. The water and sand swoosh between her toes. She can feel the wind on her skin and smell fresh saltwater as she remembers how much fun it was to pretend to fly with the seagulls. Snapping up the picture from the entry table, Emily enters the kitchen for breakfast.

CHANGE OF PLANS

"Mom, can I have this picture for my new room?" she asks.

"That's a great idea," her mom answers. Emily's tiny strands of red hair begin to lift and her eyes sparkle. "I know how much you want to start decorating your new room, but first, would you and your brother like to go to the beach today?" Slightly disappointed to not get decorating right away, she knows the beach will provide extra inspiration and ideas for her room.

AT THE BEACH

Emily's brother Nate runs after the seagulls at the beach. Emily usually joins him, but is too busy for child's play today. She sits on a large rock facing the ocean waves. This is the first time she has ever decorated a room, and she has a lot to think about.

All day long, Emily keeps changing her mind about the different colors for her room. She first chooses pink like the seashells, but then thinks green, then blue like the ocean, then purple just because. "Ah, there are so many colors to choose from. How can I ever decide which colors I want when I love them all?" On the way home she sees many more colors she loves, but the more she sees, the more she is confused. After a long day at the beach, it is a good thing the room will have to wait until tomorrow.

MOM'S ADVICE

"Mom, I'm not sure what color I want in my room and I am not sure how to decorate it. All I have is a picture of us at the beach and my magic mirror, but what else do I put in there?" Emily asks, looking puzzled.

Tucking Emily into bed in her old room, her mom answers, "You've been thinking about your new room all day. Maybe you are trying too hard. I bet if you stop thinking about it and go to sleep you might dream about it tonight." Emily nods and falls fast asleep.

15

THE BIG DREAM

As Emily sleeps, she finds herself flying through her mirror and out into a dark night sky. Flying past the moon and many stars, she lands in a faraway place all lit up like a Christmas tree, just like in her favorite book.

inspiration

shine

17

DREAM SUPPORTERS

The next morning, more of Emily's favorite things, places and people came flooding in as she remembered her dream: the Grandmother Tree in the backyard, the magic mirror, seashells, sandcastles, and seagulls from the beach, and even the colors she loves most came to her. She snatches up a pen and paper and draws out exactly what she dreamt. Her hair lifts and dances as her eyes sparkle bright.

She grabs up her idea page and runs to the kitchen. "Mom, Dad, Nate, look at my drawing! All of my favorite things came to me last night in my dream," Emily eagerly explains. "I want all of these ideas in my room!"

"That's great, Em!" her family says in unison, "We knew you would figure it out."

19

MAKING IT HAPPEN

Emily's dad, mom and brother each take turns helping Emily work on her plan for her room. They start two lists: one for things Emily already has and one for things they will help her buy. They also help her start a drawing of the room, putting the door, closet, window and all the furniture into place.

"Would you like a window bench, so you can read and write stories while you wait for the moon at night?" Emily's dad asks her. "I can build it for you."

Emily's mom asks, "Would you like your bed and the other furniture to look like they are from the time long ago you read about in your favorite story?"

"Yes, yes, oh yes!" Emily answers to all these great ideas. "And I want a soft carpet—soft, so it feels like sand." Emily can almost feel salt water swooshing between her toes.

GOING SHOPPING

Emily and her family allocate several days to finishing Emily's room. They go to different stores until they find all the right things.

At one store, Emily finds a white wolf statue in the back corner. When Emily holds the wolf, her hair dances and her eyes twinkle. "I think this wolf needs to be in your room, Em," her dad says, buying it for her.

At the paint store, the owner gives Emily's parents suggestions. But Emily already knows the colors that make her most happy are bright oranges, hot pinks, and spring greens, just like the Christmas city she sees in her mirror at night. Her favorite color, golden apricot, needs to be there, too.

Emily is getting closer to having a room of her very own. She can't stop thinking about her new four-poster bed that will be placed by the window. "I can't wait to watch the moon from my new bed," she says.

Emily's room soon fills with the colors and things she loves. Apricot walls, pinstriped curtains, and a coral pink bedcover sprinkle the room with her favorite colors. There is a pillow with seashells and a sea glass collection sitting beside her favorite books on new shelves her dad built.

24

The final touch is the wolf, placed next to the door of the room so he can protect her.

The fiery strands of Emily's hair lift and her eyes sparkle more than ever now that her room is complete. Her room, just like the magic mirror, now reflects back to everyone what Emily loves and tells a story about her.

She feels secure and surrounded by the support and dreams she needs to unlock her potential.

KATHERINE ALLEN

Katherine Allen is a holistic, Feng Shui interior designer and lifestyle coach. She is the founder of HarmoniousLivingNow.com, where she helps clients integrate the power of place and Feng Shui with the power of mindset to create harmonious and thriving environments. Katherine writes, speaks and coaches from Boise, Idaho where she lives with her husband, Jim and their daughter Serena. She is also the mother of adult children, Abel and Larissa, and a proud Grandmother of 3 beautiful grandchildren.

Learn more about Katherine's services at
HarmoniousLivingNow.com

HarmoniousLivingNow.com intregrates the power of place with the power of mindset to raise the vibration of our daily lives.

SERENA ALLEN-SZATKOWSKI

Serena Allen-Szatkowski is the creative director contributing the original story-board drawings used in the book. Starting at two years old, she began communicating with her drawings and continues to create stories, draw and design. She is now in high school and wants to pursue art when she graduates.

STEPHANIE MULLANI

Stephanie Mullani was classically trained by the top art and design schools in the world and has over 20 years of experience in illustration, fine art, and creative fields. Stephanie's work has been featured on product and package designs, magazines, and television in more than 19 countries. *Emily's Room* is the 10th book she has illustrated and was a complete joy for her to help bring to life. Connect with Stephanie at:

www.TruPublishing.com

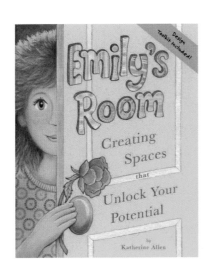

EMILY'S SPECIAL OFFER FOR YOU

Emily loved creating her very own room so much that she wants to help all her friends do the very same thing. She would love to be your friend and help you create a room that makes your heart sing, too!

All you have to do is follow along with Emily's "Lights On" Design Toolkit.

This Design Toolkit is to help you step by step create spaces that will support your dreams and allow you to bloom!

Wouldn't you like a room or a space/place within your home where your heart can sing like it did for Emily?

You'll find the same ideas Emily and her family used in this simple, yet powerful design toolkit.

Are you ready?

EMILY'S "LIGHTS ON" DESIGN TOOL KIT

LIGHTS ON SIGNATURE SYSTEM

The Lights On signature system includes seven steps to help you design a place that makes you happy, sparkle, and light up. Your room is a space that sets the intention of your dreams. It will not look or feel like anyone else's—because only you can create it from the inside-out!

Whether you are 5, or 85, the basic tenets are the same. Find what you love, surround yourself with what you love and follow what you love to do in the world. Notice what lights you up. Let these cues lead the direction of what styles, colors and textures you like to surround yourself in, remain curious and allow the adventure to begin.

The Lights On system helps you choose how to discover and identify the colors, shapes, lines and textures that brings to life your perfect thriving eco-system. This is a space that unlocks your potential, boosts your energy and raises your daily vibration. When you're finished with these seven steps, you'll have a greater understanding of what you need within a space as well as a basic plan that will help you to design from the inside out.

Let's begin.

STEP 1

FAVORITE THINGS

Write or draw your favorite things inside this heart.

Animals:

_____
_____
_____

People:

_____
_____

Things I like to do:

_____
_____
_____

Season:

_____

Places:

_____
_____
_____

STEP 2

ADD COLOR BRILLIANCE

Choose three colors you love the most.

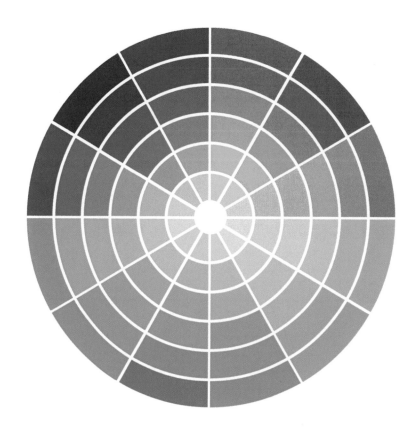

Design hint: You can create balance and harmony in your room by using the "rule of three." Pick three colors you want to use somewhere in your room. Then use one color the most, the next color much less, and the third color the least.

STEP 3

WHEEL OF TEXTURE

Texture is the way something feels. Select three of your most favorite textures:

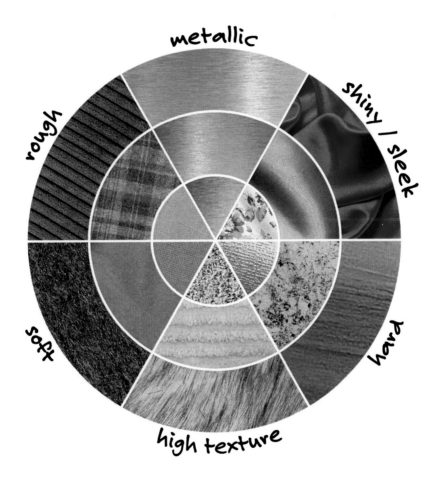

Design hint: If you are decorating a bedroom, consider the following ideas. When you climb into your bed at night, what do you want your sheets and pillows and covers to feel like? Soft, snuggly and comfortable are all good textures to have in a bedroom. Shiny and metallic can be found in picture frames and mirrors. Hard surfaces can be on the floor like wood floors or pieces of furniture. Sleek and shiny can show up as cotton sheets and satin coverlets.

STEP 4

ACTIVITY ZONES

What are the things you want to do in your room? Make activity areas in the room. Think about having a reading nook, a corner for your collections, or a place to study. Write your activity in the squares and make a list of what you need to have in order to do that activity. Fill in the blanks.

Design Hint: Keep things simple and uncluttered. Everything in your room needs to have a "room" of its own as well. Follow this simple rule: There is a place for everything, everything in its place.

STEP 5

LET YOUR IMAGINATION FLOW

Pretend this is your magic mirror. Let your imagination flow. Name the places, people, things and experiences that show up for you. Describe them or draw them in the magic mirror. Do not edit anything that reveals itself to you.

Design hint: Your imagination is real—and it can serve and inspire you in creating a room that has your unique style.

STEP 6

DESIGN PLANS

First, Draw a floor plan of your room and/or take pictures of the room.

A floor plan is a drawing of your room as if you are looking down from the ceiling.

- Label the doors and the windows.

- Draw in furniture like the bed, dressers, shelves, desk, chairs, and mirrors where you think they should be.

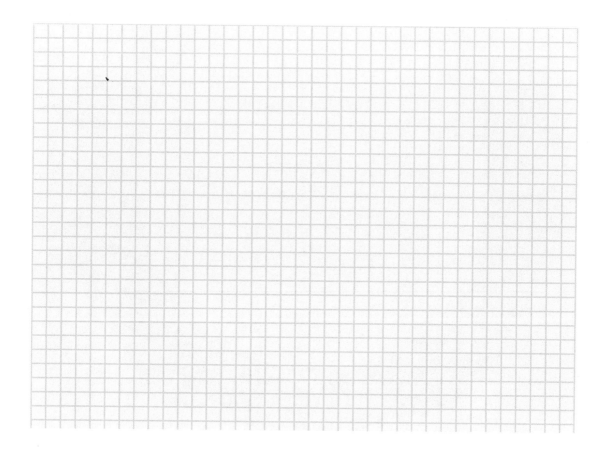

Design hint: The placement of your bed, desk and main seating areas are very important. Plan these areas so you can see people come into the room.

STEP 7

WISH LIST

Make a list of things you already have and another list of things you want to buy.

Create a folder to store your design information, such as color and fabric swatches and pictures of items that you are considering purchasing.

You now have a basic plan to start decorating a room that is all about you. Visit our website for classes and services that can further help you create environments in which you can thrive!

www.harmoniouslivingnow.com

Notes

Notes

Notes

Notes

Notes

Each square = 1 foot x 1 foot

Each square = 1 foot x 1 foot